Frankie Stein Starts School

by
Lola M. Schaefer

illustrated by
Kevan Atteberry

Marshall Cavendish Children

Text copyright © 2010 by Lola M. Schaefer
Illustrations copyright © 2010 by Kevan Atteberry
All rights reserved
Marshall Cavendish Corporation, 99 White Plains Road, Tarrytown, NY 10591
www.marshallcavendish.us/kids

Library of Congress Cataloging-in-Publication Data
Schaefer, Lola M., 1950–
Frankie Stein starts school / by Lola M. Schaefer ; illustrated by Kevan
Atteberry. — 1st ed.
p. cm.
Summary: Frankie begins his first day at Miss Wart's Academy for Ghouls
and Goblins excited and eager to learn, but when the other students tease
him for being different, he demonstrates what he already knows about being
scary.
ISBN 978-0-7614-5656-8
[1. First day of school—Fiction. 2. Monsters—Fiction. 3.
Friendship—Fiction.] I. Atteberry, Kevan ill. II. Title.
PZ7.S33233Frn 2010
[E]—dc22
2009007486

The illustrations are rendered in Adobe Illustrator and Photoshop.

Book design by Anahid Hamparian

Editor: Margery Cuyler

Printed in Malaysia (T)
First edition
1 3 5 6 4 2

mc Marshall Cavendish
Children

For Spencer, who
will be starting
school this year
—L.M.S.

To all my teachers,
especially Mr. Fielder
—K.A.

One beautiful day, Frankie Stein
came into the world.

    His parents, Mr. and Mrs. Stein, stood and stared.
Their son didn't look like them. He didn't act like them.
But as he grew, Frankie's clean-cut looks made him the
scariest Stein of all.

    And then came the day when he was ready to
start school . . .

Frankie Stein stood

on the steps of Miss Wart's Academy for Ghouls & Goblins.

He had been waiting for this night for a long time.

Frankie waved good-bye to his family and rushed inside.

During story hour,
Miss Wart read a book about ghosts.
Frankie scooted close so he could see
and hear the scary parts.

"Ewwwww," howled Wilma, pointing to Frankie.
"I'm not sitting next to him. He looks weird!"

During math, Frankie counted teeth.
"Look, Goldilocks knows his numbers!" said Skelly.

"Stop making fun," said Frankie. "I can't concentrate!"

Vinnie swooped near and asked, "Are you going to sign your picture, Pretty Boy Stein?"

The class pointed at Frankie and laughed.

"Cut it out!" yelled Frankie. "Why don't you leave me alone?"

"Because ve don't like you," said Vinnie.

"Yeah," said Skelly. "You don't look like us!"

"So what?" said Frankie. "I can still be scary, even scarier than you!"

"What do you mean?" they all shouted.

"Watch and find out!" said Frankie.

"Time for reading," said Miss Wart.

Frankie sat and read *How To Be Gross*.
Then he twisted and contorted his face
up, down, sideways, and around.
"**GROTESQUE!**" shouted
Miss Wart, and she gave Frankie a
black star.

Frankie picked up the glow-in-the-dark chalks.
He colored his face purple,
his lips orange, his fingers
yellow, and his nails black.

"BONE-CHILLING!"

shouted Skelly.
Everyone nodded.

"Time to listen to scary sounds," said Miss Wart.

Frankie listened to Coyote Calls,
then stretched his neck
and yelped so loudly
that the windows shook
and Miss Wart's teeth fell out.

"EAR-SHATTERING!" howled Wilma.

Everyone clapped and followed Frankie to
the science corner.

Frankie mixed a potion
that burbled and gurgled.
He took a big gulp and grew two long fangs.
"BLOODCURDLING!"
shouted Vinnie.

Everyone cheered, and faster than lightning bolts
the class dashed around the classroom, becoming
SCARIER and **SCARIER**.

When school was over,
Frankie rushed out of Miss Wart's Academy of
Ghouls & Goblins.

"How was your first night of school, son?"
asked Mr. Frank N. Stein.

"Ghoulish!" said Frankie.
"I heard scary stories,
counted teeth,
painted a monster,
and yelped like a coyote."

"What did you like best?"
asked Mrs. Frank N. Stein.

"Friends," said Frankie.
"I made a lot of new,
frightening friends."

"That's our Frankie," said
Mr. and Mrs. Frank N. Stein.
"A scary monster indeed!"
As the sun rose, Frankie
Stein waved good-bye
and stomped home
with his family.